MAKING SELECT

Also by Steven Barwin in
the Lorimer Sports Stories series

Fadeaway
Icebreaker
Rock Dogs
Roller Hockey Blues (with Gabriel David Tick)
SK8ER
Slam Dunk (with Gabriel David Tick)

MAKING SELECT

Steven Barwin

James Lorimer & Company Ltd., Publishers
Toronto

James Lorimer & Company Ltd., Publishers acknowledges the support
of the Ontario Arts Council. We acknowledge the financial support of the
Government of Canada through the Canada Book Fund for our publishing
activities. We acknowledge the support of the Canada Council for the Arts
which last year invested $20.1 million in writing and publishing throughout
Canada. We acknowledge the Government of Ontario through the Ontario
Media Development Corporation's Ontario Book Initiative.

The Canada Council | Le Conseil des Arts
for the Arts | du Canada

ONTARIO ARTS COUNCIL
CONSEIL DES ARTS DE L'ONTARIO

MIX
Paper from
responsible sources
FSC® C016245

Cover image: iStockphoto

Library and Archives Canada Cataloguing in Publication

Barwin, Steven
      Making select / Steven Barwin.

(Sports stories)
Issued also in an electronic format.
ISBN 978-1-55277-875-3 (bound).—ISBN 978-1-55277-874-6 (pbk.)

      I. Title. II. Series: Sports stories (Toronto, Ont.)
PS8553.A7836M36 2011   jC813'.54   C2011-903904-4

James Lorimer & Company Ltd.,   Distributed in the United States by:
Publishers   Orca Book Publishers
317 Adelaide St. West   P.O. Box 468
Suite 1002   Custer, WA USA
Toronto, ON, Canada   98240-0468
M5V 1P9
www.lorimer.ca

Printed and bound in Canada.
Manufactured by Friesens in Altona, Manitoba, Canada in August, 2011.
Job # 67772

To be good at something you have to work hard, but it doesn't mean you have to give up everything. Balance is important in life and so is standing up for what you believe in.

Thank you to my nephews Ely, Cole, and Jake and to my cousin Max who introduced me to the world of Select hockey. They answered a lot of my questions and I hope some of their passion for hockey spilled over into this book. You are all great role models for my kids, Jordan, Alisha, and Tyler.

CONTENTS

1 SELECT

The scoreboard showed the game tied at 4–4 with fifty-four seconds to go, and the pressure was on. It was only a midseason game, but in Select league, every game's important. It was halfway through my shift for the Amesbury Thrashers, and I took position on the right side of the faceoff outside our blue line.

"Let's go, Thrashers!" Coach Wilson yelled above the high-octane crowd.

My parents were to blame for most of the noise. It was easy to spot them — they were the only ones standing, clapping, and hollering. And it wasn't just because the tension in the game had risen to a peak. They stood, clapped, and hollered at every Select game. Some of the other guys on the team razzed me about it, telling me it was embarrassing for the team. But what they didn't get was that all that horrible attention wasn't for the Thrashers — it was for me. Every little bit of it.

The teenage referee held the puck above the small red circle painted on the ice. He released it and it fell to the ice. Connor, our centre and all-star captain, got his blade on it. With his wavy brown hair and permanent smirk, Connor reminded me of my cousin Richard from Chicago. Richard was the kind of kid who loved himself more than anything else, spending a large part of his day in front of the mirror. After only fourteen minutes alone with him, I usually felt like puking. That's Connor, too — he thinks he's God's gift to hockey. Bow before him or suffer the consequences.

Connor flicked the puck to Ryan on defence, before moving forward on the right wing, expecting a pass back. I hung close to the boards while Connor caught the pass and took the puck up the ice. When Connor dumped the puck behind the Flames' net, I held back, leaving it for William on left wing. William's only goal in life was to play on Team Canada and score a winning goal.

As I angled in front of the net waiting for a pass, I felt a headache starting to form — the cheering was too loud to even think. I took a quick peek at the scoreboard. Thirty seconds left.

"Tyler!" William called to me from behind the net.

When I looked at him, he didn't have the puck anymore. By the time I found it, the puck was already bouncing clumsily toward my stick. I didn't need to keep watching to know what would happen next. Up until that point, the volume from the crowd had been divided, half for us and half for the Flames. Now the sound coming from the Flames fans shook the roof.

My heart felt like it sunk, hit my stomach, and disintegrated from all the acid. The Flames player covering me had taken full advantage of my screw-up. It was amateurish, and not at all like me. How could I let the puck hop over the blade of my stick? I'd lived and breathed hockey since before I could remember — I didn't make those kinds of mistakes. Maybe I was coming down with the flu, I thought.

"Get back!" Coach Wilson wailed from the bench.

I had already turned around and was in hyperspeed mode, doing everything I could to stop the Flames player from making me look like more of a fool. "Defence!" I yelled, sending out a 911 to my teammates. One of the worst feelings in hockey is being forced to watch somebody who stole your puck on a breakaway. If I could have thrown my stick at him, I would have. I'd take any penalty, real or made up, to stop him. *Number 8, Tyler Anderson, two minutes for using your stick as a boomerang.*

The volume in the arena dropped to zero as the Flames right winger pulled back on his stick and fired it. Devon, our goalie, had come out of the net to cut down the angles. Devon was wearing his colourful mask — he'd change it if he let in more than four goals in a game, as though the equipment brought him good luck or bad. As I raced across the blue line, I saw Devon block the shot with his pads. A serge of relief rushed through me.

Then, like a bad dream, Devon went down well outside of the net. The puck somehow trickled out from under him, stopping just in front of the goal line ... and our open net.

"No!" I screamed, reaching my stick out to trip the winger or clip his stick. But he'd already flicked the puck toward our net. William slid to the rescue, blocking it with his body. The entire Flames squad stormed our net, everyone hoping to get lucky. But they were too late. Coach Wilson had called a time out.

With my helmet slung low, I made the long skate back to the bench. Even Devon passed me, leaving me feeling like a one-person parade. All eyes were on me. I could tell our guys were angry — my only saving grace was that my misstep hadn't cost us the game.

"Thank you, thank you, thank you," I offered Devon when I reached the bench.

"No problem," he said. "Just don't let it happen again!"

"That's a guarantee."

Not wasting one second of our time out, Coach Wilson barked, "You're staying on the ice, line one." Then he locked eyes with me. "And you, young man ... it doesn't get luckier than that."

I nodded, knowing it was smart to keep my mouth shut. Besides, I was man enough to admit I was scared of the coach. Maybe it was because he wore a suit to every game, like he was coaching for the NHL. Or maybe it was that his yell carried the force of a tornado. I wondered if he'd ever served in the military. And if so, how many men had he killed in battle?

With the team gathered around, the coach addressed them again: "But luck, my friends . . . luck is for losers. Talent, skill — those are words I associate with winners. Champions, even. Do you want to be losers?"

"No, Coach!" the team yelled.

"Do you want to be champions?"

I joined in when the team yelled, "Yes, Coach!"

"Then let me tell you a little something I picked up along the way. You all might find it useful if you intend on winning this one." He cleared his throat. "A good hockey player plays where the puck is. A *great* hockey player plays where the puck is going to be."

How do I do that? I wondered. *I'm not psychic.*

"You know who said it?" he asked.

No one had an answer.

"The Great One. Wayne Gretzky."

I'd had enough of Coach Wilson and his wise but predictable pep talks. They were less about motivation and more about intimidation. And he always liked to quote — or should I say steal — from great players.

"The question isn't whether you want to win or lose the game. The question is: Do you want to be the one putting the winner in the net?"

No, I thought. *The question is: Who's going to quote you if you keep quoting everyone else?*

"Now get in there and win this one!"

I turned back to the rink and looked up at the scoreboard. Twelve seconds to go. I headed out, but on the way to the faceoff in our end, Connor cut me off.

"What the hell are you doing out there?"

I shrugged.

"You usually don't screw up *that* badly. Make sure it doesn't happen again."

I couldn't help wondering if he was looking at himself in the reflection on my helmet.

"You don't just make yourself look bad, you make all of us look bad. Get it?"

"Yeah." I just wanted him out of my face.

"Play up or quit."

The ref blew his whistle. I hustled to the faceoff and took position next to a new Flames right winger. Their coach must've made the switch. You don't get a second chance after you miss on an open net.

The puck dropped and Connor sent it back into our corner. William was on it, and a Flames player was on him. Before I could jump in to help, William managed to spit the puck out. Catching it on my blade, I brought it forward, watching the Flames scramble. Once over the blue line, I took a quick peek back and saw that I had two Flames on me. I got a rowdy response when I passed the bench. It sounded like I had made it up to the coach. At centre ice, I knew I couldn't outskate both players behind me, so I veered left and crossed paths with Connor. Nearing their blue line, the coach's words ran through my mind: *Do you want to be the one putting the winner in the net?*

I fired up all the strength I had in my legs and soared ahead of the Flames defence. On a short break-away, I faked a backhander, slid the puck to the right, and flung it toward the top right corner. As I skidded to a stop past the net, I watched the puck ding off the top crossbar.

Connor swept in, scooped up the rebound, and scored. The buzzer sounded, and the Thrashers and their fans roared in celebration.

Connor bodyslammed me. "That's more like it!"

Heading off the ice, I moved past a bunch of rink chicks — girls who, for some reason, seemed to enjoy hanging around the arena. Hockey teams don't need cheerleaders, but these girls were like wallpaper around here. I recognized two of them from school. One was a girl named Claire. The taller one was Madison, Connor's younger sister, but she didn't look so cheery. As I passed by, she looked up from texting and caught me looking at her. Embarrassed, I quickly averted my glance into the stands — and right onto my mom's disappointed expression. We many have won the game, but this was not a victory to Mom.

2 THE INTERVIEW

I got my skates off and stowed my gear in my hockey bag as quickly as I could. Mom and Dad were waiting for me outside the change room. I followed them past the four NHL-sized rinks in the Vaughan Sports Village, them not saying anything to me and me not saying anything to them.

The Zamboni was already out cleaning the ice on rink number one, but the other rinks still had games in session. I didn't want to look. I'd seen enough hockey for today. I briefly wondered if we'd stop at the food stand for a Gatorade, but probably not — that meant one of us would have to break the silence.

Past the first set of doors, I watched as some poor kid skated for his life on a giant treadmill designed to handle skates. It was meant to make you a stronger skater. I remembered my first time on it. My parents had thought it was a great idea. First thing they did was tie a safety cord around my body to stop me from falling flat on my face. I had prayed that the thing wouldn't fling me off as I raced against the loud hum of the machine. Now I was used to it.

In the car, my mom was the first to speak. "So what did you think of the game, Tyler?"

I took a moment before answering the loaded question. I decided to play it safe. "I could have played better."

She chuckled sarcastically. "If that player had scored on your little misplay, we'd never be able to live it down."

As she talked, I watched snowflakes land on my window, turn into water, and trickle off the door.

"And if someone important, with any hockey influence, happened to be in the crowd … Well, I don't even want to go there."

"Uh-huh," I mumbled.

My dad chipped in from the driver's seat, "At least you got a good assist for the winner." He squirted windshield fluid and wiped some ice away.

Before I could respond, my mom replied, "But no goals in three games. That's not like you."

My goals, assists, time on the ice, *all* my stats were recorded on the league website. And my parents had it at the top of their bookmarks list. My mom was still talking, but I had a hard time focusing on what she was saying. My mind was preoccupied with where we were going, and the sports high school interview that was ahead of me.

★★★

I fidgeted uncomfortably in the seat next to my mom as we waited in a long hallway lined with chairs outside the interview room. We'd stopped for a quick lunch before my dad dropped us off at the sports high school, and the foot-long turkey sub I'd eaten was now sitting like a brick in my stomach. There were twenty or so other people also waiting for an interview. My mom looked worried, which was making me feel even more stressed. To distract myself, I tried guessing everyone's sport, but I couldn't tell the swimmers from the wrestlers.

"Mr. Anderson."

I stood up when I heard my name. "Yes, that's me."

As the man approached from across the hall, my mom threw hushed pointers at me: "Stand tall. Head up. Be confident, but not too confident. Be yourself, but don't be silly."

The man stopped in front of me and said, "I'm Mr. Connelly. Please follow me."

Walking behind him into the classroom, I couldn't help staring at his buffed, bald head. Mr. Connelly took a seat and gestured for me to sit in an empty chair across from the three other adults already seated.

"I am the head interviewer," Mr. Connelly began, "and I'm also joined by two of our teachers — Physical Education and English." The teachers nodded their heads once as he introduced them. "Each of them will ask one question."

I nodded, taking in the high school classroom. It looked better than my school, mostly because there were a lot of new computers with flat-screen monitors. The ones at my school were ancient.

The gym teacher spoke first. "On a scale of one to five, with five being the highest, how would you rate your hockey skills?"

I replied with one word. "Five."

"Why?" he asked.

"Because I've been playing hockey for a long time and I'm always working on my skills. I play both Select and house league, and compared to the guys I play with . . . well, I think my coaches would tell you I'm one of the top-ranked players." I took a breath, realizing I'd spat out my answer too quickly.

There was a short pause. Then the English teacher fired her question at me.

"What historical or fictional character would you most like to be, and why?"

Panic sparked in my brain. They weren't asking any of the questions my mom and I had prepared for.

Stalling for an idea, I let out a thoughtful, "Ahh." Then I remembered a book I had signed out from the school library for a biography project. "Mario Lemieux," I said. He may not have been my favourite player of all time, but I happened to know a lot about him from my project. "Mario is someone I look up to because of his amazing hockey achievements. He won six Art Ross trophies, which means he scored the most points in the league six times. Mario also won three Hart trophies, two Conn Smythe's, two Stanley Cups, and an Olympic gold medal."

I paused and noticed that they were nodding, which seemed like a good sign.

"But what's really amazing about Mario is that he never reached his full potential. He wanted to beat all of Wayne Gretzky's records, but he got sick and had to stop playing. Who knows what else Mario could have achieved if he'd had the chance?"

My throat was dry and I had started sweating. But I felt really good about my answer. One more question and I could get out of here.

Mr. Connelly cleared his throat and asked, "What is something you'd like to change about the world?"

Brutal question, I thought. I felt like I was in a beauty pageant. Not knowing what to say, I started to talk about Africa and the starving children. Looking at all the computers in the classroom, I somehow rambled my way into saying we should get more computers to the children of Africa.

Mr. Connelly stood and I followed him out. With the letters of recommendation from my coaches, I should have felt more confident than I did about getting in. But at least I had survived.

★★★

The moment I got to school the next day, my best friend Glenn was all over me. He had a thousand questions about my interview. Going to a sports high school would be Glenn's dream, and it felt like he was forcing me to relive it just so he could experience it himself. I was relieved when the end-of-lunch bell rang.

"What classes do we have this afternoon?" I said to change the subject.

"English and History."

I pulled the two binders out and slammed my locker shut. But as soon as we started walking to class, Glenn began drilling me about the interview again.

"Look, I don't know if I got in. Guess I have to wait for the call."

"All the coaches love you," Glenn said. "Your application is gold. I'd be shocked — like, I won't believe there's a God — if you don't get in."

"You believe in God?"

"Yeah, the god of hockey. I'm on the fence about the other one. Fine, I'll give up on hockey if . . ."

"You like hockey more than food." I laughed.

"The only thing that sucks about you getting in is that we'll be going to different high schools next year."

"That does suck, but I haven't gotten in yet."

"Stop being so negative."

"I don't really think I have a choice, anyway. I *have*

to go to a sports high school, even if it means moving cities."

"Sounds like your mom talking."

Glenn and I shared a laugh. He knew how intense she could be.

He added, "Well, she *can* be a bit much."

"That's a nice way of putting it," I added. "She's pushing to get me High Performance Athlete status."

"Oh yeah? What would that get you?"

"It means that I'd get a guaranteed spot. Plus I'd get special recognition, and more flexibility on tests and projects if I'm away at tournaments."

"That would be incredible. Sounds like celebrity status."

"I don't think it's that big a deal."

"Dude, you're totally underplaying this opportunity. I'm jealous."

I let out, "Don't be," without looking at him.

"What's going on with you? You should be jumping up and down!"

"Can we just change the subject, please?" I asked.

"Sure. Man, I was so psyched by our last game, I couldn't sleep."

I was hoping for a subject other than hockey, I thought. We were in such different places. He was still in hockey la-la land and I was living in hockey reality — the main difference being that for him, hockey was still about having fun. For me, it was about scoring, winning, and my point count. According to Coach Wilson and my parents, there was no point in playing the game at all anymore without those. Even house league was stressful for me because the coach expected all Select players to reach their four-goal quota for the team. Like if you didn't, you should feel embarrassed or something.

"You're pissed off with me."

"I'm not, Glenn! Just forget about the sports high school and the interview. Move on!"

After a pause, Glenn said, "I think we have a real chance at making the playoffs this year."

His words were grating. He was my best friend, but I couldn't relate to him at all anymore. I took a deep breath to calm myself, and then said, "For me, that would be kind of a nightmare. The longer house league goes on, the busier I am, because it ends up overlapping with Select finals. And then there'll be summer hockey camp."

"Yeah, I guess I didn't see it that way."

A voice rang out from behind me. "Hey, Tyler!"

I turned around to see Connor and his groupies from Select. Alone, each of the guys was pretty cool, but something annoying happened when they got together.

"Hi. What's up?" I responded.

Connor put his arm around my shoulder and turned me away from Glenn, like he wasn't even there. "You're lucky you manned up with a good pass to me last game or Coach would have come down hard on you."

"Yeah, you don't want to mess with Coach," Devon said. "I once let a long-shot goal in while I was busy cleaning the ice in my crease, and during practice, he made me clean the dressing room with a toothbrush."

I rolled my eyes. "No, he didn't." But I wasn't so sure ...

Connor took his arm off my shoulder. "Just get your game up."

Not that long ago, Connor and I had been pretty good friends. He would invite me to his house, and we'd play Wii and hang out. As soon as my game started to slide, though, the friendship ended, and he'd been riding me ever since.

I nodded my head, looking back at Glenn. I felt worse for him. Every year he tried out for Select and he never made it. Maybe it just wasn't in the cards for him. *Big deal*, I thought, *Select isn't the be all and end all.* But it was like Glenn was holding onto something just out of reach, and it was hard to watch sometimes. He shot off ahead of us.

"So did you go to your interview yet?" William asked.

"Today. You?"

"I'm not interviewing."

I continued walking to class, wondering, *Why not?* Unfortunately, the first thing I thought popped out of my mouth. "You giving up on hockey?"

Connor and William laughed at me in stereo.

"No, stupid," Connor said. "We both got High Performance Athlete status!"

"I'm guaranteed in," William added.

"Congrats," I said, half jealous and half not caring.

Our English teacher, Mr. Cavanaugh, came out into the hall just then. "Okay, everyone. You've got me now. Stop talking and get in line so we can go in. We have a lot of work to do."

I stood wedged between William and Devon, while Glenn stood at the front of the line next to the new ESL student. Maybe Glenn wanted to be in Select so badly not only because it was a better level of hockey, but because it came with a better social life . . . that is, if you wanted it.

3 HOUSE

The puck trickled behind our net, spun, and stopped dead, and that's where I got my stick on it. Scanning left to right, I patiently waited for someone to get open. All of my Lions teammates seemed to be out of position or covered by Hawks players. Coach had me play defence this game, to challenge me. He said someone with my skill set — whatever that means — should learn that the best offence is a strong defence. And he's right. As opposed to left wing, where I'm always hunting for the puck, playing defence means I'm always looking to feed someone the puck. The game's laid out in front of me, and I can just hang back and create a play. Coach could just as well have put me in net or as a bench warmer, though. My parents wouldn't even care, because *it's only house league*. I was always a lot less stressed at Tuesday night house league, and even though I was playing in the same arena as my Select games, it felt totally different. Mom or Dad would drop me off at the front doors and pick me up after the game at the same spot. That freedom was the best part.

"Tyler!"

I looked up at Glenn, who I would've passed the puck to, but he had a player stuck on him. Instead I passed it down the boards, hoping maybe a Lions player could get free. Almost immediately, I had to move forward to support, but by the time I arrived, the puck was still free, sitting against the boards. Easy pickings. Securely on the blade of my stick, I waltzed the puck over the blue line, toward the red. Over my shoulder, I saw that my wild and crazy manoeuvre had ruffled the Hawks' feathers, and they scrambled back after me.

"I'm up your right side!" Glenn announced.

"Gotcha!" I responded.

Ahead of me, my only obstacle to the net was a huge Hawks defender. I knew from how swiftly he switched from skating forward to backward, that he was a Select player like me, slumming it in house league. I cranked up my desire to succeed in this game and locked eyes with him, preparing to deke. If somehow I didn't make it, Glenn would be there to pick up the rebound.

Gripping my stick tighter, I shuffled the puck back and forth on my blade to determine which side to take the Hawk. Nearing the top of the faceoff circle, I faked right and then took the more difficult path, sliding between him and the boards. I was at a bad angle to the net, so he didn't even see me coming. *Everybody goes up the middle*, I thought. The bad angle didn't bother me today. I hit the brakes hard, sending shards of ice spraying into the air.

The Hawks player was left fumbling to stop, and I was left with a clear shot on net. I adjusted my angle to an easy forty-five degrees to the net, and I could smell a goal. For a split second, I went back and forth — slapshot or wrist shot? Deciding on an up-close slapshot, I dug my skates into the ice, pulled my stick back waist high, and unwound. Just before making contact with the puck, a thought dawned: I had already reached my four goals per game maximum. *Too bad house league doesn't keep stats online. Then my parents would have nothing to complain about,* I thought. Knowing my goal wouldn't count, I snapped a pass to Glenn, who took advantage of the goalie stretched to his max across the crease and pushed the puck into the net.

The buzzer belched and our yellow goal count changed from four to five.

The Hawks coach yelled, "Time, ref!"

Glenn reached out for a gloved high-five. "Awesome pass!"

"You're the one who put it in the net." He butted helmets with me in celebration, and we turned toward our bench. "Nice one."

"Not as big a deal if I had scored it during a Select game. I was *so* close to making Select this year." Glenn held two gloved fingers apart. "I missed it by this much."

I nodded and thought, *Yeah, but you miss it by that much every year* — but I would never tell him that. Three years ago, Ms. Kowalsky's seating plan had made us best friends, and I'd always felt bad that I had something he really wanted. Glenn was a pretty good hockey player, but every year he missed the Select cut. My dad called me a prodigy, and I always wondered why Glenn couldn't be one too. He practised just as hard as I did. Was it the way I was raised? Was it because there are pictures of me as a two-year-old holding a hockey stick? Hockey just seemed easy for me. I wished Glenn could be the same.

Back at the bench, Coach Yeung called, "Gather round, boys."

I reached over the boards for my water bottle.

"Good idea, Tyler. I want everyone drinking lots of water, replenishing their fluids."

He clapped his hands together once. "Who's having fun?"

I couldn't help but compare Coach Yeung to Coach Wilson. Coach Wilson would never ask his team if they were having fun.

Everyone kicked their skates loudly against the boards and replied, "We're having fun!" I followed the group, enjoying the enthusiasm.

"Good to hear. The game's a close one. We're only leading by one. And that's okay — we're doing our best out there. I like everyone's hustle." He rubbed his hands together for warmth. "Who remembers my three hockey rules?"

Someone shouted out, "Do your best, do your best, do your best!"

Coach Yeung was like a warm blanket. He never yelled, and always made everyone feel good. He seemed to love hockey without the worry of winning. Maybe he could speak to my mom.

He continued: "That's right. This is a heated game. Just make sure you" — he deliberately slowed down each word — "do . . . your . . . best!"

Heated? I looked up in the stands. The fans weren't divided. There was no one yelling at the players or the coaches. People were drinking hot chocolate and chatting to each other. Of course, it may just have been calm because my parents weren't there.

The ref blew his whistle, signalling the end of the time out, and the coach pulled our line aside. "Just get the puck to Tyler," he said, half-jokingly.

I dropped my head in embarrassment. I hated the way that sounded. I rolled my eyes so Glenn could see, and wondered how that had made him feel. Skating to the faceoff circle with Glenn in tow, I held my stick up and pointed with it to the rest of our line. "Look at them. They hate me."

"Why would you say that?" Glenn asked.

"Because of what the coach said." I did my best Coach impersonation, lowering my voice so it was deep and quiet. "'Get the puck to Tyler.' He made it seem like I was better than everyone else."

"Hate to break it to you, Tyler, but you *are* better. It's why you're in Select."

I took my position on the right side of our net. With only two minutes showing on the scoreboard, the ref released the puck. Adam, playing centre, won the draw and flicked it back to me, following Coach's orders. Stepping forward with the weight of the puck on my stick, I decided not to play along. I quickly passed it back to Adam. He was one of the biggest guys on the team, and I always found it funny that he played centre. With his size, he'd be better suited for defence. Adam wasn't expecting my pass, and he spun around like a figure skater, searching for the puck. When he found it, he returned it back to me, and a horrible game of hot potato started. *At least we're running down the clock*, I told myself. Keeping to my strategy of not letting the coach make me feel like a standout, I fed the puck back to Adam. In an instant, things turned horribly wrong.

"Cover him!" our goalie screamed.

It was too late. The Hawks centre had swooped in, picked off my pass, and delivered it up high and into the right corner of the net.

Our goalie hadn't stood a chance.

I felt the heat of all the Lions' eyes turning to me. I bet they were all thinking, *How could a Select player not see that coming? Idiot! Moron!*

I could feel Coach Yeung watching me all the way to centre ice. He didn't have to say it; I knew I'd made a major mistake. That Hawks player saw me making the pass long before I had even made the decision. Guess that's what Coach Wilson had been talking about. *Be where the puck's going to be.*

Glenn called out to me, "You okay?"

Looking up at the stands, even the laid-back crowd took notice. "I don't know what's wrong with me. It's like I'm on a bad luck streak or something."

"No such thing as bad luck."

Coach Wilson's words came to my mind again. *Luck is for losers.*

Glenn didn't give up trying to make me feel better. "Everyone goes through it. Even the great ones."

I nodded, not buying a single word. "Maybe." I took a deep breath and looked at the time on the score-board. One minute, nine seconds glared back at me. I shouldn't have let the coach's words get to me. Now I had to make it up to the team. I felt my heart race out of control and sweat pour down my face.

The ref dropped the puck and Adam took posses-sion of it. There was no time to waste. He looked back at me. I couldn't believe that even after my screw-up, he'd still consider sending it to me.

"Get open!" the coach yelled. It was the first time I'd ever heard him raise his voice above a library tone.

"What the —" I blurted, as two Hawks attached

themselves to me. They knew it was going to come back to me! But even though I was being double-teamed, Adam still passed it over. My stick was held down and I was blocked. I watched, helpless, as the puck sailed through my legs. Glenn moved in and used his body as a blockade, allowing me to break free of my captors.

Way outside his crease, our goalie, playing both goalie and defence, snatched the puck.

Quick check: *Scoreboard's running down from forty-four seconds.* I chewed it over in my head. *They want me to win it for them. Why fight it?* "Give me the puck," I ordered.

With a player already on him, our goalie flipped a pass over the heads of three oncoming players. I blocked it with my gloved hand. This time, I wasn't going to give it up. Over the red line, my Hawks cover scrambled to lock me down again. No use — I was long gone. I counted down in my head, *fifteen . . . fourteen*, leaving a ten-second buffer for a rebound if I needed it. Crossing the Hawks blue line, I centred myself to the net, leaving me lots of room to go either way. *Time to make my move.* Looking right, I went left, then cut sharp in the opposite direction. Crossing the crease, the Hawks goaltender folded to the ice. Smiling at the open net, I flicked the puck up in the air — but somehow he got his blocker up to deflect the shot. The crowd echoed my disbelief. How had I missed it?

I was right of the net, and the puck was nestled at the boards on the opposite side. The scoreboard hurried down from six seconds, and I knew I couldn't reach the puck in time. I was out of luck. I slammed my stick onto the ice as Hawks players surrounded me in celebration of coming back and tying it up. I didn't want to go back and face my bench. Coach would probably say that a tie is respectable, but I didn't want to hear that. Glenn found me in the crowd, but I didn't want to face him either. I was officially cursed.

4 CHARMED

After dinner, I scavenged through my bedroom looking for a good-luck charm. I pulled a shoebox out of my closet. Taking the lid off, I uncovered hundreds of hockey cards. It was a serious hobby that I'd started when I was four. Flipping through the cards, I looked for one that might stand out. Many of them were in bad condition, torn or folded. I stopped at a Sidney Crosby card. It was a cool card, but I was hoping for something different, like a rookie card of someone who went on to break NHL records. I tossed the card back in the box and flipped faster through the deck. I stopped at a rookie card for Ryan Miller in a Rochester Americans jersey. The back of the card said the Americans were the Buffalo Sabres rookie team. He won forty-one games, tying Gerry Cheevers's record. I looked at the front of the card. *He's a goalie. I don't need good luck being in net. I need luck scoring on net.*

I ditched the box back in the closet, closed the closet door, and went to my trophy shelf. I laughed out loud when I thought about what I would look like walking around everywhere with a good-luck trophy. I needed something small. Then I found it. I pulled an MVP medal off the shelf and blew the dust away. Perfect.

A vibration from my cell phone shot down my leg from my pocket before it started to ring. "Hello?"

"You're not watching hockey with your dad, are you?" Glenn asked.

"Surprisingly, no. What's up?"

"Just calling because I have a question about the test."

"Test? What test?"

"The His-to-ry test." He chunked it out into syllables like I was stupid.

"Man, I totally forgot."

"Well, I guess you can't help me with my question then."

"I paid attention in class. Hit me with it."

"How did the doctrine of manifest destiny affect Confederation in Canada?"

I thought for a moment. "Well, Confederation ..." I thought some more. "Confederation is ... I'm screwed."

"It's only ten-fifteen. You have time to study."

That was a sign of a good friend: not rubbing it in that he was prepared and I wasn't. "Test day might be a good day to fake the stomach flu."

Glenn laughed. "Has that *ever* worked with your

mom? Remember that time you had stomach cramps and she still sent you to school?"

"My appendix burst!"

"Exactly!" he said.

"You have a good point." I thought for a few seconds before continuing. "I could Google an illness she knows nothing about."

"You could also study."

"Now you sound like my mom."

"Just study and call me if you have any questions about Confederation."

"I do have one question."

"Yeah?"

"What's Confederation?"

Glenn laughed. "Confederation means —" he began, but hung up mid-sentence.

I guess I deserved that. I looked at my backpack lying on the carpet next to my desk. It was screaming at me, *Time to study!* Ignoring its whine, I flopped onto my bed. The wallpaper and matching duvet I've had since I was a kid was a repeating pattern of blue and red hockey players. I closed my eyes and allowed my mind to drift, wondering why my game was sliding. I opened my eyes, taking in the giant Team Canada poster above my bed and the two rows of shelves weighted down by trophies collected over the years. My eyes focused on a Most Valuable Player trophy from the Select league last year. My mom was happier than I was when I got it.

She told everyone, even strangers in the mall about it.

My phone vibrated on my bedside table, moving one of my many hockey Bobbleheads. I turned onto my side. It was a text from Glenn saying, *How's it going?* I didn't respond. Wayne Gretzky, in Bobblehead form, nodded his approval from the bedside table. I wondered if he'd ever had bad luck on the ice when he was my age. Did he ever get into a slump? Probably not. He's scored more goals than anybody else in the NHL — 894. There's no way a legend like that ever had to worry about his game. *How'd he do it?* I wondered. I wasn't expecting an answer from the god of hockey or anything, though that would make my life easier. *What am I thinking?* I flicked his head and watched it bobble around again before pulling my head off the pillow and sitting back up.

Trying to shut hockey out of my mind, I opened my backpack and pulled out my history binder. I flicked a puck with my picture on it off my desk, then started to study. *I should have taken better notes,* I thought, straining to make sense of my own handwriting. I flipped through a couple more pages, and it was pretty much the same story. Eventually, I swiped my binder onto the floor with the hockey puck and pulled the textbook from my backpack. It wasn't only heavy, but thick, too. I had a mountain of reading to do if I was going to catch up. I scanned the table of contents and a found the chapter I was looking for: "The Road to Confederation."

Focus, I ordered myself. Scanning the chapters and sub-headings, I found a section on what Glenn was asking me about — the doctrine of manifest destiny. I ran my fingers along the words to help keep me on task. The words *expansion* and *across North America* stood out. I heard the door handle turn, and I looked up at my mom as she entered my bedroom without knocking.

"Studying?" she asked.

No, I thought to myself, *I'm fishing.* "History test."

"Mind if I interrupt with very good news?"

I turned in my chair. She had my attention and, truthfully, I wasn't going to complain about the interruption.

She entered my room and sat on the edge of my bed. She spoke softly. "I just received an e-mail."

I nodded, playing along. *I get twenty e-mails a day. What's the big deal?*

"You ready?" The excitement on her face was impossible to miss. She wore an *I just won the lottery* smile.

I nodded again.

"The e-mail said that an opening came up and you get a spot to try out for Double-A hockey!"

My eyebrows lifted and my stomach sank. More hockey was not what I needed.

"Tyler? You don't seem very excited."

"I'm just tired."

"Your father and I are proud of you." She put her hand on my shoulder. "Honey, this is what you've dreamed about since you were six. Each step forward you make, you get closer to junior hockey, a college scholarship, and the NHL draft. This is such a great opportunity for you."

I smiled at her. "Playing for Dad's favourite team, the Red Wings, would be amazing."

"That's the spirit. Now let's talk about this week's hockey schedule."

She began to run down my week, dividing it into games, practices, Select, and house league. I wondered what life would be like on an AA team. The games and practices would double, I guessed. Plus, I'd have to drop house league and abandon Glenn. As she continued to run through my schedule, I looked down at my textbook. I was getting more tired by the second, and it became impossible to focus on anything. My eyes began to feel heavy. I needed to crash.

". . . And we'll worry about next week later. Okay then? Good luck with your studying."

Staring down at my textbook, I felt her quick kiss on the top of my head and heard my bedroom door close. The words in front of me seem to blur together, and I began to wonder how soft my textbook was. I lowered my head, and soon found out that it wasn't soft, but it would do for a pillow. With any luck, the words would magically jump off the page, crawl through my ear canal, and plant themselves in my brain.

5 WALK THE PLANK

"You had me fooled," Glenn said with a smirk. "I thought you actually had the guts to play sick."

Before I could respond, Ms. Lee announced, "Okay everyone. Up you go for 'Oh Canada.'"

The anthem started and I got to my feet. The annoying country-music version they were playing lately was just a painful fifty-five-second wait before a test I was going to fail. I just wanted to get it over with. The anthem ended and Ms. Lee was quick to roll the tests out.

Glenn leaned my way and whispered, "Good luck."

I nodded, avoiding eye contact. He didn't need to look a dead man in the eyes. If I didn't pull this off and the sports high school asked for another round of updated marks — which would make my first-round marks look like I'd cheated — my parents would have my head on a platter.

"Tests are out. Name and date them and get it done." She returned to her desk and put her feet up.

I flipped mine over. Adding my name and date was the easy part — so far, I'd gotten a perfect score. Looking around the classroom, it wasn't hard to sense that I was slowest out of the Confederation gate. I reached into my pocket and touched my MVP medal. I didn't think even a good-luck charm could get me out of this test.

First question: *Define manifest destiny*. How did Glenn know? Next question: *Describe free trade*. I knew that in hockey, teams made trades. I also knew there was a deadline and that some players were free agents. Connecting it to history would be tougher. A horrible feeling of being off-course washed over me, and I put my pencil down. *Who am I fooling? I don't know this stuff.* To my right, Glenn was madly writing down his answers, looking like his brain was out-racing his hand. A lot of other people were doing the same. A voice rang out, jarring me from my daze.

"Mr. Anderson."

It was Ms. Lee, and she didn't sound happy. She got up and started to march toward me.

My first thought was, *What's her problem?*

"Do you have a wandering eye problem?"

I knew enough not to respond.

She stopped in front of my desk, breathing heavy and looming over me. "I don't tolerate cheaters."

I couldn't prove it, but I'm sure I had a deer-caught-in-the-headlights look. *Cheat? Me?*

"I told everyone on the first day of school that cheaters will be prosecuted."

All eyes were on me. I felt like shark bait. "Ms. Lee, I wasn't cheating!"

"You were looking at other people's papers."

"I wasn't! I swear!"

"I know what I saw."

I stood up. "Ms. Lee, you're wrong."

She pointed a finger at me. "I don't like your tone."

"This isn't fair!"

"I've heard enough from you." She grabbed my test. "Go to the office!"

I stood frozen for a moment, thinking maybe she'd change her mind.

"Go!"

Guess not.

I stormed out. Traipsing down the hallway, I dragged my feet past classes in session. I'd done this walk many times, but it was usually to the washroom or the water fountain. My anger at how unfairly Ms. Lee had treated me boiled over inside, and I couldn't hold it in. I planted my left foot, drew my right one back, and released it into a blue recycling bin with everything I had.

The bin tipped and paper spilled onto the hallway floor. I let out a frustrated sigh and looked around. If any teachers had witnessed my outburst, then I'd be in even more trouble, and possibly even suspended for damaging school property. I took a quick look over my shoulder, and right into a pair of blue eyes. It took a second for me to realize it was only Madison, one of the rink chicks.

I moved quickly downstairs, toward the office, and noticed that Madison was following me. *Was she going to report me?* I entered the office and was told to have a seat. Madison sat one seat over from me. I shuffled uncomfortably in my chair.

"Relax, it's going to be a while," she said.

I nodded and returned to my angry gaze. After a moment, I said, "I shouldn't be here. I was wrongly accused."

"We all are," she replied.

I looked at her, not knowing how to take her comment. Her jeans were very ripped, and she didn't seem to care much about how she looked, compared to most girls in grade eight. She wore a white t-shirt with long green sleeves poking out underneath. The words on her shirt were covered by her long, black hair.

"What are you in for?" she said with a grin. "Littering?"

I smiled. "Accused of cheating on a history test. But I'm innocent; I didn't do it." The last part was loud enough for the secretary to hear. She scowled.

"Aren't you going to ask about me?" Madison asked.

"I was getting there."

"Sorry, I'm not a very patient person. Anyway, I pushed a boy away who was coming on to me. He didn't get the message until I whipped a basketball at his head." She paused. "And unlike you, I'm guilty as charged."

"I'm getting the idea that this is not your first time sitting here."

"Why would you say that? You don't know me."

I held my hands out, defensively. "It's just that you're so calm. I'm shaking." I held out my hand so she could see.

She smiled. "Yeah, I've been here before. But all for good reasons."

"I'm sure."

"So here's the deal. There's a big difference between the VP and the big P." She smiled at her little joke and I smiled back. "If you're lucky, you get the VP. It probably means a slap on the hand, a warning."

"And the big P?"

"That's if you're unlucky. You don't get to the big P without going to the VP unless you really crossed a line."

Just then, the doors to the VP and big P opened. I slid my hand in my pocket and touched my MVP medal. I was about to get a second chance to test my good-luck charm.

I was called to the VP's office and Madison was summoned to the principal. Not only did I get out of the test, but I was about to get off with just a warning. For just a second, I hoped the principal wasn't going to be too hard on Madison.

6 OPPORTUNITY KNOCKS

"I can't believe he made us do laps." Glenn's face was fire-engine red, and sweat poured down his forehead like rain on a car windshield.

"Nothing I'm not used to," I said, slipping my Nikes on.

"I think our gym teacher gets off on seeing us run in circles. All he does is sit on the bench and count the laps."

"I guess so."

"You okay?" Glenn asked.

"Yeah, why not?"

"Nothing, just wondering."

I waited until we reached the top of the stairs on the second floor to answer his question. I knew he wouldn't let it go, and I hadn't exactly been upfront with him about what was bothering me lately. "Well, I guess I'm worried about my History mark. Plus I've got Double-A tryouts coming up. And ... if I make it ... then I'll have to give up house league."

"That would suck. But hey, NHL, all the way. I hope to join you at some point, if I can catch up."

"Well, it's just that —" We were interrupted when I heard my name called from a small group of girls passing by.

It was Madison. "How's it going?"

"Okay."

I stole a look at Glenn. He seemed surprised. I hadn't told him about talking with Madison in the office. I used to tell him everything.

"Well . . . see you later," she said.

Before the pack of girls headed off, one of them said to Madison, "Did you invite him?"

Madison slapped her arm.

I didn't know exactly what was going on, but I figured she was trying to embarrass Madison. A long, awkward pause wedged itself between us.

Madison broke it. "It's nothing. Just hanging out with some friends tomorrow night."

I didn't know what to say. She wasn't exactly being clear. "Oh."

"If you want to come, you both can."

Madison's friends laughed, and she threatened one with another slap.

"But hold on a second, who are you anyway?" she asked, finger pointing at Glenn.

Glenn was looking down at the floor, clearly embarrassed that she didn't know his name. I answered for him. "This is Glenn. She's Madison."

There was an awkward silence. "Uh, I've got Double-A tryouts really early Sunday morning. Thanks, though," I finally said.

She smiled. "Anything that early has to be awful."

"It's a hockey tryout," I added.

"Well, it's no big deal." She continued, "We should go." The pack of girls shuffled away, giggling and shoving each other down the hall.

"What the heck was that?" Glenn asked.

When I shrugged my shoulders, Glenn turned and walked away from me.

★★★

I had never met another Canadian who loved an American hockey team more than one in Canada. That was my dad — the biggest Detroit Red Wings fan ever. Guess that's how it works when you're from Windsor. He told me that he'd been so close to the United States growing up that he could see it from his bedroom window. He laughed when he told me that it was either a short drive or a short, cold swim to Detroit.

Dad and I were sitting on the basement couch while two announcers tried their best to make the play-by-play sound more exciting than the Detroit-Toronto game on the television really was. I was rooting for the Leafs, but I didn't make it public. I never did. My dad took his Red Wings hockey seriously. He hated interruptions. He even hated if the phone rang during commercials.

"Did you see that?" Dad said suddenly, almost jumping out of his seat.

"What?" I looked up, not really into the game.

"You didn't see that play? Are you blind?"

He might have mistaken my blank gaze at the television for me actually being into it. Seeing the pros play only reminded me how bad my game had been lately.

"It looked like Draper was going to shoot, but then he faked it, swung around, and passed it right across the crease."

"Did anyone score?"

He looked at me like I was from Mars. "No."

"Oh."

"I'll show it to you later. I'm recording it."

You record and catalogue every game, I thought.

"You should try that next time you have the puck in front of the net without a good shot."

I said, "Sure," like it would be no big deal.

"Hey, boys." My mom entered the basement stirring milk into a cup of something hot.

"Detroit's winning," my dad announced.

"Uh-huh." Even though my mom over-managed my hockey career, came to all my games, and shouted my name from the stands, she hated watching hockey on television. It bored her. She told me that she'll start watching it when I'm playing for an NHL team. She once told me that she'd prefer it to be the Maple Leafs so she wouldn't have to travel far to see me. "I just got off the phone with Coach Wilson. He said you didn't mention that you were trying out for Double-A."

"I must've forgotten to tell him."

"You should have. He's very proud of you."

"Oh, and another thing." My mom tested her drink, and I could tell it was too hot because her glasses fogged over. "I picked up some new skate laces for you. They're sitting on your bed."

If I make Double-A, I thought, *she's going to become even more of a micromanager. Telling her I want to skip the tryout might destroy her.*

"Ooh," my dad cringed. "Check out that hit."

I turned to watch the replay. A Red Wings forward performed a menacing bodycheck on a Leafs player, sending him into the boards.

"Got to keep your head up," my dad said.

"I can't watch this anymore," my mom said. "I'm heading upstairs."

My mom left, but my eyes were fixated on the Leafs player who had to be hoisted back to the bench. *That's one way to get out of hockey,* I thought.

7 THE DILEMMA

A blow of the whistle by the referee and a knock on my helmet by the coach, and I was thrust back into the game in front of me. I got off my butt, dragged my legs over the boards, and stepped down onto the ice. I looked up to read the scoreboard, needing a reminder of what was going on in the game. Period two. Score tied at 4–4. I used the information to determine that it was a heated game.

"Let's do it, guys!" Connor yelled out.

Standing to the right of the faceoff circle in our zone, I checked out the player next to me in a Falcons jersey. *Oh yeah. We're playing the Falcons.* I glanced over at Connor, bursting at the seams to get his stick on the puck when it dropped. Looking back at the bench, I saw Coach Wilson shaking his head at the third line as though they had offended him. Even higher, in the roaring stands, were the eager parents and family members waiting for their kid to score a goal so they could parade around in celebration with the head of the goalie fixed to the top of their sticks.

I don't want to be here anymore, I told myself. I wanted out — by any means. But I knew the hockey game would only stop if the arena was struck by a tornado, or a flash flood or, even better, an earthquake.

The crowd's volume increased sharply.

The puck dropped and there was no sign of a natural disaster to save me. The defence fetched the puck and I skated along the boards, not wanting the puck, but not wanting to look like I didn't want it.

"Get a move on!" Coach Wilson yelled.

Yeah, yeah, I thought. Behind me, a Falcons forward tried to knock the puck loose from William, and an idea entered my brain. Lightening may not strike on command, but an injury — real or fake — could pull me out of the game, or at least give me a time out from hockey. I burned away the few remaining minutes of my shift, not really accomplishing anything.

Back on the bench, I pushed away the coach's voice and used the moment to plan my escape. I quickly ruled out faking an injury. If I couldn't get the flu past my mom, what would she do with a knee injury? I'd probably find myself dealing with doctors in a hospital, and that would be a disaster. I scooted along the bench toward my next shift, looked up at the game, and thought: *I need to get injured for real.*

Connor bumped me with his shoulder pad just hard enough to get my attention. "What the hell were you doing out there?"

I played dumb. "What?"

"Coach may not see what you're doing, but I do."

How could he know? "I'm not doing anything," I said defensively.

He leaned in closer to me, face mask to face mask. "You're staying back for the puck so you can bring it up and score."

"That obvious?" I asked, enjoying a moment to have fun at Connor's expense.

"Defenders know who's centre and who's captain. They're not going to pass it to you and you're not going to bring it forward. That's my job."

"We'll see," I responded, smiling.

Connor turned away in frustration, and I went back to planning how to get out of playing the rest of the game.

The end of the second period was in sight, and I joined my shift on the ice. *If I'm going to get injured, I need to make sure it doesn't look like a set-up.* On the ice, my Thrasher defenders brought the puck forward. While they passed it back and forth, I devised a new game strategy. Now I wanted the puck more than ever. And I let my team know, shouting, "I'm open!" even though it was already on its way to Connor. He drove it into their offensive zone, and I yelled again, "I'm open!" even though I really wasn't. Not having a shot, he passed it to William on left wing. Connor was ignoring me and I wasn't exactly surprised, him not being my biggest fan. I banged my stick on the ice, calling for the puck.

The coach ordered, "Take the shot!" On the opposite side of the rink, William obeyed the coach, wound back, and fired one at the net. He missed.

The puck whirled along the boards, and I went to fetch it in the corner. With my stick on the puck first, I spotted an oversized Falcons defender on my tail. *This is my opportunity.* Wedging the puck between my skates, I waited for the Falcons express train to smash me into the boards. *Injury, here I come!* The crowd was yelling at me to get the puck out of there and not to freeze the play. I turned around and found myself at eye level with the Falcons jersey logo. *Wham.* The Falcons player knocked me down with a concrete thud. Winded but struggling for air, I squeezed my eyes closed. *This is it*, I thought, *exactly what I asked for.* I heard voices and opened my eyes to see Connor and Coach Wilson peering down at me.

"You okay, buddy?" Coach asked with concern. "Don't you worry about it. That guy's getting at least two minutes for roughing."

I nodded, still trying to locate the coordinates of my injuries. Connor continued to stare down at me, fulfilling his captain duties, but probably hoping that I didn't get up. *That makes two of us*, I thought, almost letting out a crack of a smile.

A referee joined the coach. "He's going to have to try and get up."

They held out their hands and I grabbed them, using them as cranes to support my weight. Shaky, but on my skates, a horrible feeling spread like wildfire across me. *Nothing hurts.* I wasn't injured. Just as that started to sink in, loud applause — a standing ovation from both sides of the audience — poured down onto the ice. They had united just for poor me. And I knew that the coach had figured out I was okay when he told me I'd have to get back on the horse.

8 THE CONNECTION

Outside the change room after the game, I was leaning with my back up against the wall when Mom and Dad found me. They were quick to get on my case.

My dad rarely threw the first punch. "I've never seen you play with your back against the action like that," he said.

But his words were tame in comparison, just a set-up to my mom's volley of accusations. "It baffles me, too. Is that how you think you play hockey?"

I stared down at the dirty floor, dodging their fiery eyes. *What would they say,* I wondered, *if they knew my mistake was planned? That I was playing out most of the game, waiting for my moment.*

"You're just lucky you didn't get hurt," my mom said, with a grain of concern. But then she ruined it with, "I'd hate to have to cancel that Double-A spot I worked so hard to get for you."

"Thank goodness," my dad added. "Are you still sore?"

"I'm okay."

Dad reached for my duffle bag. "Let me take that for you."

It was on wheels, but I still thanked him.

The change room door opened, spilling out William. His parents approached mine, and they started with some small talk, then got right into reviewing the game — minute by minute, play by play. I took the distraction as an opportunity and slid away along the wall before William's parents got to the part about how badly I'd played. Slipping out of the cramped hallway, I stepped into the arena and took a deep breath. I was trying to calm myself after having my head inside the lion's mouth. At least my mother didn't bite down this time. I felt a strong desire to disappear, or at least hide. I took the stadium steps two at a time and found a spot on the bench in the last row before the rafters. I needed another lung-filled breath, and I took two. "Stupid, stupid," I said aloud, as I thought about my failed attempt to get injured.

"Tyler?"

I looked around, trying to locate where the sound had come from.

"Over here."

From around a large green beam that ran from the ceiling to behind the seats, I saw Madison.

I waved, trying to figure out if she was spying on me. She got up, jumped a row down to avoid the beam, and then stepped up and sat beside me. She was very close, considering there was no one else around.

"How's it going?"

"Okay," I said, with zero enthusiasm. I stared down at the freshly cleaned rink.

She broke the ice. "You look like you're hiding from someone up here."

I was impressed with her psychic abilities. "You know, it's a great sport from up here. Not as complicated as down there."

"Hockey?"

Okay, maybe not psychic. "Yeah."

"I hate hockey."

I replied, "I've never heard someone say that before," only realizing afterward that it had made me smile.

"It's true. Hockey's possibly . . . no, it *is* the most boring sport on the planet."

My smile bloomed into a laugh.

"I'd rather watch cars going around in a circle three hundred times than suffer through a hockey game."

"And I thought you were a rink chick. So you're here just for your brother or something?"

"Hell, no. I'm here because my parents promised sushi for lunch after the game." She moved her hair away from her eyes, tucking it behind her ear. "So who are you hiding from?"

"My mom. She's trying to be my manager." I looked away from the rink for a moment and glanced up at

Madison. "It's complicated."

She smiled. "When it comes to parents, you have to lay down the law."

"You don't know my mother."

"When my parents were on me about my grades, I threatened to get a piercing."

I laughed hard. "That's pretty harsh."

"You've gotta show them who's boss."

I thought for a moment about what would happen if I actually did that. I wondered how quickly I'd be sent to live with my eighty-year-old grandmother. "Thanks for the advice."

"It's more than advice. It's words to live by."

I turned my whole body toward her. "So you really hate hockey, huh?"

"Big time. Why are you smiling?"

"It's just . . . I don't know anybody else who hates hockey. It's funny."

"If you don't like hockey, then you shouldn't be playing. This should be the happiest time of your life."

"It should?"

"When university hits, it's all work, sagging skin, then the slow ride to retirement and death."

I loved her dramatic overkill. More importantly, I found myself laughing . . . in a hockey arena.

She stood up, ready to go. "You coming to hang out tonight?"

"I don't know."

Madison leaned down and gave me a kiss on the cheek. "What about now?"

9 BREAK FREE

After my historically bad history test, telling my mom that I was "going to study at Glenn's house" on the eve of Double-A tryouts had only been successful because she was happy that I was trying to get my marks back up.

So now I sat in the basement of a house I'd never been to before, on a very comfortable couch, feeling overwhelmed by the number of tech toys in the room. All the big brand names were represented. About fifteen or so people were spread around the basement. Some were on the couch, some were playing video games, and two people I sort of recognized from school were playing at a foosball table. To say the house was ginormous was an understatement. It was a monster, with more washrooms than my house had rooms. And the only studying going on was Glenn wanting to know more about Madison. I was there . . . well, for the exact same reason. I didn't want to miss out any more on the so-called "greatest years of my life."

"So, Tyler."

I turned to Alexander, the kid lucky enough to be born into this royal family. He had curly red hair, which almost matched by his bright orange Chuck Taylors.

He continued, "Don't think I've ever seen you outside of school."

"Hockey," I replied, because it said it all.

"That's right. You're an all-star or something."

"Or something."

He laughed, then got up off the couch and turned the background music up, washing out the sounds coming from the video games. I felt the music's heavy beat.

Next to me on the couch, Glenn cleared his throat, anxious to get through the rest of the twenty-question interrogation he'd started on the walk over to find out why I hadn't told him about Madison. I'd tried to explain that I barely knew her. The only thing that had shut him up was when we turned into the enormous driveway and saw the size of this place . . . Both our jaws had dropped with envy.

"You showed!" Madison flopped onto the couch, close enough for our legs to touch.

"Yep," I said. "I'm glad I came." I looked around the room and was happy that no one from Select was here.

"What about you, Glenn?"

He said, "Yeah," and then pounced. "So, you hate hockey?"

I shook my head at him. Whatever he had gotten

out of me, he was going to use against her. I shouldn't have told him anything.

"It's not my thing," she replied.

"You should see Tyler play. He's gonna go all the way."

I didn't know if it was just jealousy driving him, but he needed to stop talking like that.

Madison smiled. "Are you his manager?"

Glenn fired back with, "Are you his girlfriend?"

The question hung in the air. It caught the attention of everyone on the couch. I jumped in to put out the fire. "Glenn, can I talk to you?" He followed me to the corner of the basement that housed workout equipment. I leaned on the treadmill and said, "Why are you being like that?"

"I'm not being like anything. Just making conversation. I want to know who she is."

I whispered, "She's Connor's younger sister," from the corner of my mouth.

"What!" Glenn's expression was wide with surprise.

"It's no big deal."

"Sorry. I just can't believe it. So what *should* I talk about?"

"I don't know — just not Madison!"

"Okay."

That's it? "Okay," I replied. "Let's just . . . chill and have fun."

On the way back to the couch, he asked, "You

psyched about your tryout tomorrow?"

I stopped him, my hand to the middle of his chest. "And I don't want to talk about hockey either."

"Why?"

"What's your problem? I just don't want to, okay?"

"Okay, okay. Not wanting to talk about hockey doesn't make any sense to me. But if you say so."

I might as well have told him I don't want to talk to *him* anymore.

Back on the couch, Alexander had started pouring drinks. He asked, "This, this, or both?" In his left hand was a bottle of Coke. His right hand held what looked like a bottle of alcohol. Almost everyone squished on the couch said *both*. When he got to Madison, she was quick to say both as well. Following her lead, I held up two fingers for both and avoided a glare from Glenn, who was attempting to make me feel awful for having fun. Madison clinked plastic glasses with me and I took a sip. The drink was strong and hardly tasted like Coke at all, except for the bubbles. In between songs, the basement was quiet for the first time. I noticed Alexander's ears perk up when he heard the basement door open.

When he said it was his dad, I panicked. I took my drink and swallowed it in one gulp. When his dad appeared at the bottom of the stairs, I smiled and let out a small burp.

"Everything okay down here?"

Alexander said, "Yes," and we all nodded in unison.

"You still want me to order those pizzas?"

"Thanks, Dad."

"No problem."

His dad left and everyone broke into quiet laughter. Alexander stood up and asked, "Who's ready for a refill?"

I raised my glass first, eager to try and see if alcohol would take away all my thoughts about hockey. With any luck, soon the H-word wouldn't even be on my mind. Tonight was going to be a good night.

10 PLANS ARE MEANT TO BE BROKEN

A puddle of saliva had formed on the carpet, and it wasn't until I saw the horrible reaction on my mom's face that I realized I was lying on the floor in my bedroom, still dressed in last night's clothes.

"What are you doing on the floor?" she demanded, as she flicked on the lights and violently ripped open the curtains.

My brain was slow to process what she was saying — sort of like my dad's old computer in the basement that gave me time to make a sandwich, get a drink, and throw a few text messages out before it booted up. *I feel horrible,* I thought, as though waking up on the carpet wasn't clue enough. I didn't know alcohol could do this to someone. With a hoarse voice, I tried to cover up the crime scene. "I was studying at Glenn's house."

"I know where you were. What time did you get home?"

"Umm . . . I don't remember the exact time."

Not pleased, she laid out her demands: "I need you

downstairs and ready to roll in eight minutes."

I looked at her for a long second, wondering what was up with the big rush.

"Double-A tryouts," she barked in a loud enough voice to wake the neighbours.

"I know," I said, trying to be convincing.

"Eight minutes," she repeated.

When she finally went downstairs, I raced to the bathroom and dropped knees down, face hovering over the toilet bowl. I opened my mouth wide. Nothing. "Please let me throw up," I prayed quietly to any god that would listen. My head was spinning and my stomach was twirling. A knock on the door startled me and I jumped to my feet. "Yeah?"

The door swung open. It was my dad, in the middle of an eyes-closed, enormous yawn. "Ready to go? We only have four and a half minutes left . . ."

★★★

With the craziness of last night still swirling around in my stomach, I did my best to keep to my mom's schedule. Rushing into the change room, I looked around for a spot to get changed and found a small space in the corner. Almost everyone had their gear on already. While I did my best not to throw up, Dad swiftly got me dressed and into my skates.

"I still think you look green," Dad said. He patted

me on the back. "Just a little nervous energy, right?"

I nodded, flumping back down on the bench and resisting the urge to close my eyes. I scanned the quiet dressing room, taking in the competition. *Having my first hangover probably puts them at a big advantage,* I thought. I wanted this over with. If I had the power to fast forward, I would.

Dad's voice broke the silence in the room. "Where's your stick?"

"Oh, no."

My dad jerked up, and the motion made me feel sick. "You forgot it? I'll go check the car." He took off and I lowered my head.

Could I really have forgotten my stick?

★★★

I stood unsteadily on the ice holding a donated stick. My parents were embarrassed enough that I forgot mine, but while my dad drove back home to get it, my mom had to ask to borrow one from another player's mom. I did a couple laps, trying to shake off the cobwebs in my head.

Three coaches — two men and one woman — dressed in matching coach gear took control from centre ice. I stood in the second row, pleased that no one else from Select was here.

The female coach cleared her throat. "Most of you

won't make the team."

I sensed everyone else was holding their breath with me.

"Even so, never give up. My name's Coach Moore and these are Coaches Duval and McGuire."

I watched and waited for them to take a bow or something. They didn't.

"We're starting with a scrimmage game. Show us your best stuff, because we will be watching you."

As if on cue, Duval and McGuire broke off in opposite directions and began to hand out pinnies. I slid on a purple pinny, and tried to keep my stomach from turning.

Coach McGuire announced, "Purple, north end. Red, south end."

I didn't know north from south, so I just followed the purple jerseys and took the left wing slot because, by the time I arrived, it was the only spot available.

Coach Moore held the puck up in line with her head and yelled out for everyone to listen. "No periods here. First to three goals wins." She dropped the puck without any warning, and a thought jumped into my head: *"Puck" isn't that far away from "puke."*

Our centre won the faceoff draw and the puck was flung back to our defence. I meandered my way up the left side. *Drinking and skating definitely do not mix.*

Once I got over the Reds' blue line, I wondered why it was so quiet. I turned back only to see many red jerseys attacking our net. On my way back to help, I scoped out the three coaches. They were preoccupied with the game action. I don't know if they saw that I had zero game in me. By the time my skate crossed our blue line, the red team had already scored.

"Two more to go for the red team," Coach Moore broadcasted.

I skated back into position and wished there was a line change. I looked over at the bench — it was empty. In the stands, my mom caught my attention. She mouthed what looked like, *What's wrong with you?* I shrugged back. Then she frantically started pointing at me. I turned around to see the game was back on.

Back in our net, our goalie slapped his stick on the ice to motivate us — *or maybe just me.*

Taking in the other players, I thought, *Everyone here wants this more than me. I should be jumping up and down to be here.* Instead I felt burnt out, like I had reached my peak. I understood for a moment what Glenn was going through. He wasn't making the Select team because his playing wasn't getting any better. My game hadn't just stopped getting better, though. It was going down fast.

"Tyler!"

I looked up into the stands at my mom, who was screaming my name. *What's up with her?* I wondered. Feeling a tug on my stick, I spotted the puck resting on my blade. What happened next felt like slow motion. It started with a large figure appearing in the corner of my eye and travelling fast — too fast for me to react. Like in an animated flipbook, I saw myself from outside my body, watching. With every flip of the page, the figure drew nearer. I wanted to call, *Watch out!* to myself, but that would do little good. I knew what was on the next page. I imagined my brain emitting an emergency warning to any parts that were vital to my existence — heart, stomach, spine . . . *bail!*

Whoop!

My right shoulder took the first impact, sending my body into motion. Problem was, my head took a moment to follow. I felt my neck slingshot forward and my legs begin to crumple. All my pain sensors went into overload.

The last page in the flipbook closed and time returned to normal. I saw my reflection in the Plexiglas, and suddenly I was back inside my body. Shutting my eyes, I braced for impact with the boards. I realized then that my plan to get injured was only good in theory. In reality, I hadn't really thought things through.

The impact was not where I had expected. My right knee made contact with the boards first. I rebounded off the boards and grabbed at my knee, in excruciating pain. Then I was flat out on the ice.

"Looks bad."

I squinted my eyes open at the sound of Coach Moore's voice. She asked, "Are you okay?"

What a stupid question!

Coach McGuire followed with, "Where does it hurt?"

Another moron question! "My knee! Aughhh!"

"What we're going to do," Coach Duval said, "is get you up."

The two male coaches grabbed hold of me under the armpits. "One, two, three." They hoisted me up and I winced in pain, putting all my weight on my left skate. I was startled by a small round of applause from the players. They looked at me, and I could see on their faces what they were thinking: *Poor guy's not going to make the team.* Through my pain, I looked at them and thought, *Poor suckers, one or two of them are going to make the team.*

★★★

One of the other parents had offered to drive me and my mom to the hospital, which was how I ended up in a car, still in my skates, holding an ice pack on my throbbing right knee. My mom hadn't said a word to me other than to tell me she'd called Dad. Would she punish me for getting injured?

At emergency, Mom filled in the X-ray consent form, still without having said one word to me. The ice pack, now melted, felt like warm water in my hands, and I fiddled with it, nervous for my X-ray. I was angry at myself, because though I hadn't tried to get injured on purpose this time, I knew I'd screwed up. Sitting in the hospital wasn't a perfect escape plan.

My name was finally called and I followed the nurse, hopping into a small room overcrowded by a large X-ray machine.

A nurse asked, "Are you comfortable?"

"Yes," I lied. My knee was very sore. Under the X-ray machine, with its beams firing silently at my right knee, I took cover, protected by a very heavy lead apron. I lay there confused as to what a big knee injury might mean for me. *Will I not be able to play hockey, ever?* That's not what I wanted; I'd just needed a break, a time out. *What if it's permanent? Will I ever be able to play other sports?* I felt my heart rate double, and my mind raced along with it. *Will I have to drop out of the sports high school, if I even get accepted? Will I have a limp?*

After the X-ray, my dad showed up. "It's going to be okay, Tyler," he said, and reached for my hand.

"You're sure about that?" my mom asked.

He was smart enough not to answer.

"I'm going to leave it to the professionals to tell me whether to be positive or not. And right now, it does not look good," she continued. "I want the best sports medicine doctor to give us a second opinion."

I slunk back in the bed.

My dad was about to say something, but was interrupted by a doctor carrying a black-and-white picture of my knee.

11 DOWNTIME INTERRUPTED

"Relax. Glenn gave me your number. So what did the doctor say?" Madison asked. I pressed my cell phone closer to my ear because of all the loud background noise from the students around her.

"She said I was lucky I didn't break anything."

"So you're okay!"

"Well . . ." I kept an eye on the door from my bed. "She said I bruised my knee."

"That doesn't sound too bad."

"I know, but it still hurts."

"How long are you out for?"

"I was told to rest for a few days, and then take it one day at a time."

"I'm sensing that you're not too happy about that."

"Enough about me. What's happening at school?"

"Here? Nothing. Teachers are still annoying. Students are even more annoying. We had a stupid lockdown, but sadly there was no real threat."

"Just a drill?"

"Yep. I have a few more minutes left of lunch."

"Where are you?"

"Well, I'm supposed to be in the washroom, but I'm hiding in the stairwell."

I laughed.

"You're not missing much. Wish *I* bruised my knee."

"I might have to hang up quickly if my mom comes upstairs."

"Is she that scary?"

"In this house, it's her way or the highway, so what choice do I have?"

"Haven't you been listening to me? Take control."

"It's easier said than done."

"The first time, yes. After that, it's not so bad."

"So you're in control?"

"Pretty much . . . and I have a lot more ammo, if needed. But it's different for you."

"How?"

"You've got a lot to catch up on. You've been a good kid for far too long."

Footsteps rang out from the hallway, and I barely got out, "Gotta go," before my mom entered my room.

"How's it going?"

"Okay." I was amazed at how quickly she could move. I shifted in my bed to avoid sitting on my cell phone.

"You look uncomfortable."

I nodded.

She handed me a glass of orange juice and a blue pain pill. "It'll help with the swelling."

I took the submarine-shaped pill and swallowed it, followed by enough OJ to drown it.

She sat on the edge of my bed, careful of my right leg. "We also need to do some of those stretches."

I pushed myself further up on my pillow. "I'm kind of tired."

"It's not an option if we're going to get you back on the ice." She pushed up the sleeves of her sweater beyond her elbows. "Bend your knee."

I did, and was sad that it didn't hurt so much anymore.

She pressed her hands on my knee and slowly pushed it toward my stomach. "How is that?"

I scrunched my nose. I wasn't going to go through all this trouble to just end up back on the ice. "It hurts." I desperately needed to ride this out.

With her hands, she continued to push my knee back. She asked, "That hurts?" Then she continued without waiting for me to respond. "You've made a lot of progress. I'm amazed at how far you can bend it back."

"Well, it still hurts."

She stretched my leg out so it was flat on the bed and stood up. "You're recovering very quickly. I'm going to book a checkup appointment for tomorrow." She smiled. "And I want you to start walking around today. Get used to putting some weight on it. Come down for lunch. I've got it ready for you."

I just wanted her out of my room so I could go back to being miserable. I wondered what Madison would do in this situation. Tell her to shut up? How would I get her to back off — threaten to get a tattoo if she pushed me to get back on the ice?

★★★

For the next few days, I felt forced into eating lunch downstairs in the kitchen. I gobbled down the tuna sandwich and handed the empty plate to my mom, who stood at the sink.

"I'm going out for a bit. Would that be okay?" she asked.

"Yes." *It would be more than okay.*

"And when I get back, we can do some more stretches."

"Sounds fine." I watched her grab her keys and her purse, and I let out a massive sigh of relief when the front door finally locked. I propped my feet on the coffee table and flicked the television on. Between talk shows and game shows, it only took a minute before I realized just how bad daytime television was. I settled for some action movie that looked like it was made twenty years ago. By the time a commercial hit, I was bored out of my mind. I stood up and was surprised that I could put pressure on my knee. I reached for my orange juice on the table and spotted a picture of my mom during her gymnastics days. She was doing an amazing backward arch on a balance beam. She looked so happy. I wondered why she never talked about it.

12 CLIFF DIVING

A half-hour later, my cell phone vibrated in my hands. It was a new text message from Madison that read, *Has big bird flown away?*

I laughed, typing back, *lol. Big bird's gone, all clear.* I sent the text, got off the living room couch, and moved to the front door, opening it.

"Hi." Madison smiled. She had her hair in two braids and she was chewing gum.

I said, "Hi," checking over her shoulder to see if my mom had suddenly decided to cancel her plans. Madison slipped out of her boots and followed me back to the couch. The smell of cherry gum filled the air around me. "Did you bring a lunch?"

"Ate it on the way here." She tapped my right knee. "You look all better."

"Had my follow-up appointment this morning. Doctor said I'm okay to play tomorrow night."

"Again, I'm sensing this is bad news."

I didn't respond.

"Most people are happy to be able to walk normally again."

I scraped my teeth over my bottom lip.

"You're holding back on me. If you don't want to talk about it, that's okay, too."

"I hurt myself —"

"I know."

I looked down and said, "On purpose." She didn't respond, so I looked up at her.

I noticed she had stopped chomping on her gum. I felt like an idiot. My body was trying to make me cry, but I held back, forcing my eyes not to embarrass me. To cover it up, I stared at the coffee table and started to rant: "I wanted a break from hockey and I didn't know how else to get it. I tried to figure out different ways, but with my mom pushing and pushing, I had no other option. I had already tried it in a game, leaving myself open for a hit. I got taken down pretty hard, but not hard enough. Then, at the Double-A tryouts, I was looking for a way out and I guess it found me. I got bulldozed into the boards and ended up damaging my knee, but obviously not enough. I tried twice and couldn't even get injured properly." I took a breath. "I've been miserable and losing sleep over this and blaming everything in my life on my mom and hockey. Stupid, right?" I looked away from the coffee table, turning toward Madison. "You don't know how good it feels to just say that. To let it out. Admit it."

"It takes a lot of guts to try and hurt yourself."

I nodded, not knowing how to take her compliment. The house was quiet for a moment, and for the first time since meeting her in the school's office, I felt uncomfortable around her.

"I've done a lot of stupid things to get back at my parents, but yours beats them all!" she said.

I laughed to cover what I was really wondering. *Was I injuring myself to get out of hockey, or to get back at my mom for forcing hockey on me?* I didn't have an answer.

"Your mom must've been pissed you didn't make the team."

"Very. She's still holding a grudge against me, though she won't admit it. I could hear her yelling at my dad. She was taking it out on him."

"Parents are clueless," Madison added. "Oh," she said, as though an idea had landed on her head. "Forgot to tell you. You asked me to explain to Glenn why you weren't at school, and I did."

"What did he say?"

"Nothing, really."

"I don't know what's up with that guy. All he cares about is hockey, like he's going to make it to the NHL or something. I think he might love hockey even more than my mom does. Maybe he can move in here, and I'll live in *his* house. His parents actually do normal things, like go to the movies."

"That's sad."

"I know, right?"

"Not him. I'm talking about you." Madison stood up. "You need to stop giving in to everything they tell you to do."

"How?"

She pulled her cell phone from her pocket. "Lunch is almost over. I need to get back for classes."

"Come on, you can't leave me hanging like that. You're the pro at this. When I try to talk to my parents, I don't know what to say to get them to listen."

"This isn't just talk? You're willing to confront them?"

"I tried to break my leg! I'm desperate, and more than ready."

"Okay," Madison said enthusiastically. "It's about time. Let's take back your life!" She started to move around the room. I stood up, excited.

"You failed the first step, but that's okay. At least you tried. Trying to hurt yourself was genius — well, more like mad-scientist genius. You should have done something like that a long time ago. You've given them the ability to walk all over you, but we can jump-start this."

"Great," I said, clapping my hands and ignoring the butterflies in my stomach. "Maybe hockey wasn't that —"

"You're going to need to confront them and tell them what you want. Go into the kitchen and come back. Pretend I'm your mother."

I stepped into the kitchen, walked around the kitchen table, and went back into the living room. Madison caught me off guard. She had her hands on her hips, and the look on her face was stern.

"What do you want, son?"

I burst into laughter, bending over and holding my stomach.

"Do you want to do this or not?"

"Okay, okay." I stepped into the kitchen and pivoted around back into the living room.

Madison wore the same expression. "What do you want, son?"

About to laugh, I looked at the picture of my mom on the side table. It stopped me. "I want to take a break from hockey."

"Excuse me?" Madison asked, playing my mom.

"I'd like to stop playing Select — just house league from now on. And I'm not so sure I want to go to a sports high school."

Madison released her arms and broke from character. "Don't say *I'm not so sure*. Tell her *you don't want to*. Tell her what you want!"

"I don't want to go to a sports high school. I just need a break."

Madison shifted back into character. "I always knew you were lazy."

Her harsh comment took me by surprise. "Well —"

"Be strong!" Madison urged.

"I'm not lazy! Maybe —" I stopped myself. "I'd just like to lose the insane schedule and have time to do normal things."

"But hockey's the only thing you're good at."

"Why won't you just back off and leave me alone!"

Madison broke from my mom's character, smiled, and said, "That's better! Now it's time to take control. Let me — *her* — have it. Yank that Band-Aid off!"

"I don't know what to say."

"You'll think of something in the moment. Don't plan anything. The piercing thing was something I came up with on the spot. The point is, I followed through with it. I called their stupid bluff, and now they don't question when I say something because they know I'm going to do it." She lifted her shirt a little to show off her belly button ring.

I nodded my head, wracking my brain for something to bite back with. The piercing line wouldn't work, because I didn't want to have to get one.

"I'm late for school. Are you ready, or are you going to wimp out?"

"Ready!"

Madison dug her hands into her hips and stared at me for exactly twenty seconds. I know, because I counted every one. "You're going to take a time out on hockey after all the work I put in? Early mornings, years of expensive equipment, and now you don't want to play anymore? Where would I be if I was a quitter? Why don't you go to your room and think about what you're doing and who you're affecting when *you* decide that *you* don't want to play hockey."

I stood frozen. Madison was good — *too* good.

She took her finger and pressed hard into my shoulder. "What are you waiting for?"

I let the words bulldoze out of my mouth, unedited. "If you don't listen to me, I'm going to quit hockey and . . . become a figure skater."

Madison stared back at me.

"What? It was the first thing that came to me."

And then she cracked up, breaking character. "That was great! That was so funny, but you said it so seriously."

"You think it will work?"

"Yes. Now I'm *really* late for school."

I walked her to the front door. "You were so good as my mom. And you had all the hockey details."

"Remember, my brother plays hockey, too."

"I almost forgot about Connor."

She turned to me before leaving and said, "Tonight's the night you take your life back."

★★★

I didn't say a word during dinner. I just squirmed in my chair, not knowing when to have *the talk*. Anxiety built up inside me as I went over and over the dramatic skit with Madison in my head. *Things would be so much easier,* I thought, *if I just ignored what I was feeling and moved on with my life.* Madison was right about me never standing up to my parents. My whole life, I have always been agreeable. Take the garbage out — sure! Mow the lawn — why not! I needed to show them that I was somebody they couldn't push around. The word *Band-Aid* came to mind. *Pull it off like a Band-Aid,* I told myself. I looked at my dad across the table. He was busy twirling his spaghetti onto his fork. Maybe I'd wait until my mom took a mouthful, so I'd have a few seconds before she tried to bite my head off. Looking at her plate, I saw it was empty. *Do it!* I thought, as though I was trying to push myself off the side of a cliff. *Tonight's the night I take my life back!*

First, get their attention. I dropped my fork and it clanged against my plate. *Second, let them have it.* "Guys —"

My mom interrupted, "I hope you enjoyed your dinner." She stood, grabbed my plate, stacked it under their plates, and put them in front of me. "Please take these to the kitchen."

I nodded, picked up the plates, and dragged them to the kitchen sink. I put them down, stopped for a second, and turned back to face them. "Mom and Dad, there's something I need to talk to you about."

My dad looked up from his glass of iced tea, but my mom didn't even bother turning around.

She spoke first. "Tyler, it's been a very long day. A very long week, in fact, with the hospital and doctor's appointments. We can talk another time." She got up and walked behind me, to the sink.

My dad said, "It *has* been a long week," giving me a crooked smile.

I moved to the living room, pulled out my cell phone, and sent Madison a text: : (

13 GAME PLAN

"Last night was a disaster!"

"I can't believe how tough your parents are." Madison pulled her hair away from her eyes and tucked it behind her ear. "They're starting to make mine look cute and cuddly."

I checked out her t-shirt. It was black with a red stop sign on it. Inside the sign, it read: *What are you looking at?* "I can't let them have it; I can't even talk to them. They just don't listen."

"I underestimated them."

"That's okay," I said. "Now you understand exactly what I'm dealing with."

"So what does this mean? You're just going to give up?"

I looked back at Madison without an answer. "I don't know what to say. I mean, I've got a game tonight, and things are going to go back to normal."

"I didn't take you for a quitter. There are other ways around this." Madison turned to Glenn. "Your friend's doing battle against his parents, and he's losing. Any bright ideas?"

Glenn looked past me at Madison. "Not sure if *friend* is the right word."

I jumped at Glenn's comment. "What's your problem?"

He stared at me for a moment before turning to Madison. "The only way he has a chance in hell of going up against his mother is to go through his dad. His mom's mean. His dad's a lot less mean." He shoved his locker door shut and turned to leave.

"Wait!" I grabbed his shoulder, stopping him.

He barked back, "What do you want?"

"That's a genius idea," I said. "Wish I thought of it."

Glenn glared at me. "Can I go now?"

"Not until you tell me what's wrong."

Without hesitation he replied, "You shut me down at the party, and since then, you've barely even talked to me. And you clearly don't want to talk about hockey, but you won't tell me why."

I mumbled, "You wouldn't have understood."

"Plus, I really haven't seen you since you became friends with Madison." He turned to her. "No offence."

"No problem." Madison smiled back. "I'm going to go. You guys talk this out."

"No!" I snapped back. "Look, Glenn. I'm sorry. Okay?" I didn't wait for him to accept, just in case. "And about not wanting to talk about hockey . . . I've just been feeling burnt out. It's been hockey twenty-four seven for as long as I can remember, and I need a change."

"So are you really quitting hockey?"

"I'm not quitting. I still love the game. I just want to play without all the stress."

Glenn nodded his head, taking it in. "And me wanting to talk about it all the time doesn't help."

"That's what I've figured out. It's not you — it's me. It's my problem. I see you playing and I know you're actually having fun. No one's counting your goals or, even worse, the goals you should have had. I want that kind of hockey back."

"And this is what you've been battling over with your mom."

"Yeah. But every time I've tried to initiate battle, my mom's shot me down."

There was a moment of silence. It felt great to clear the air with Glenn.

Madison stepped forward. "Now that the soap opera's over, can we do something about it?"

Glenn and I nodded.

"Good. I say we go with Glenn's idea of splitting your parents up so you can talk to your dad first."

Glenn added, "Tyler, your parents do everything together. When are you going to get a chance?"

"Want to come see my Select game tonight?"

Glenn's eyes lit up. "That would be cool." I probably

should have invited him before.

"What about you, Madison?"

"As much I hate the game, my parents would be thrilled if I showed interest in watching my big brother play hockey."

Glenn laughed.

"I love it when you trash talk hockey," I said.

Madison smiled. "So, Tyler, tonight's the night you take back control of your life."

I nodded. "Yes. And if anything happens to me, Glenn, you can have my hockey equipment."

"Thanks?" Glenn responded.

"And what do I get?" Madison asked.

"Ahhh . . ." I tried to think of something funny to say. Something Madison-worthy.

Glenn jumped in for me, "That box of love notes you wrote her!"

14 POWERLESS

After being on the disabled list, it felt strange to load my hockey gear in the car and drive to the arena. It felt even stranger to know that Glenn and Madison were waiting for us. The fact that I was about to get on the ice again didn't even cross my mind. I was too focused on the plan — and what would happen if it went horribly wrong. My eyes caught the top of the arena, and the car pulled into the parking lot. I took a deep breath before unbuckling my seat belt and stepping outside. I grabbed my duffle bag from the trunk and slung it over my shoulder. Each step toward the rink doors made my stomach turn. I tried to think of ways of stalling, but came up with nothing. I felt like I was standing on a conveyor belt. I was standing still, but the ground beneath me was moving, pulling me forward.

My dad stopped. "Hold on."

"What is it?" my mom asked.

"Tyler, aren't you missing something?"

"Huh?"

My dad shook his head at me. "It's made out of wood, and you put tape on it . . ."

"Not again!" my mom barked.

My dad pulled my stick from the trunk. "Here you go."

"Thanks." I took the lead, stepped up onto the curb, and entered the arena's sliding doors. It was rush-hour busy in the arena. I passed by rink one on the left and rink two on the right. Number one was in the middle of a team practice and number two had little kids learning to skate on it. I pushed away the memories of me learning to skate here. At the halfway point, in front of the snack bar and with the other two rinks ahead of me, I paused, waiting for the cue.

A voice rang out, "Ms. Anderson! Do you have a second?"

I knew it was Glenn's voice. The question was, did she?

"Probably something about the arena budget meetings tonight," my mom grumbled.

She didn't know it was Glenn!

"I'll be a second. Why don't you go ahead," my mother said, following the voice.

My dad started to walk, but I stopped.

"You okay?" he asked.

I nodded and prepared to tell him everything I was

feeling. I had practised what I was going to say all night, and now, somehow, I had forgotten my lines.

"That was silly." I was shocked to see my mom return so quickly. "There was no one from the hockey board there." She looked at me and my dad for a moment. "What are you two waiting for? Tyler has a game to play."

★★★

Geared up and on the ice for my first shift, I glared down at the ice, thinking about my failed plan to free myself. Going through my dad hadn't worked, and now I was at a total loss. *Sucks being me,* was all I could think as the puck dropped at centre ice. I gave the scoreboard a once-over. The Spitfires had us down by one already — not that I cared.

The puck caught my attention as it grazed past me. A Spitfire defender whipped the puck over our blue line and into the corner. I turned sharply and headed into our zone for some support. My shift had just begun, but the feeling of not wanting to be here washed over me. I felt doomed, on the ice and off. My mom always refused to listen to me. She just didn't get me, and somehow she'd got my dad on board. Even after all of Madison's guidance, I didn't know if I could face her again.

William shot back on defence, scooped the puck

out of the corner, and looked to make a pass to me. Bad idea. My head wasn't in the game. In fact, it was trying to get out of the game. I wasn't ready at the blue line when the puck came my way, and it got picked off by a large Spitfires forward. I trailed behind him as he brought the puck, centring it inside the blue line. All I could do was watch as the puck sailed through traffic and found the top-right corner of the net. Devon didn't stand a chance.

The Spitfire celebrated the goal and then brushed past me, as if to shove it in my face. My instinct was to shove him back.

He stopped and said, "You got a problem, loser?"

"Actually, I do." I swung at him, pushing him out of my personal space. He stepped closer. My next swing was less of a push and more of a punch. He pushed me back and I thought, *An injury might not work, but a fight could*. I dropped my stick and grabbed his helmet, pulling him into a headlock. He tried to wriggle out of it, but I held on. His gloved hands jabbed at my stomach. He was hard to keep in the headlock, so I used my weight and dropped him to the ice. Out of the corner of my eye, I noticed that both benches had cleared. The two referees looked busy trying to stop other fights from breaking out. I heard heavy breathing as the Spitfires player tried to claw his way out from under me. My equipment did little to stop him from striking me with a series of quick jabs to my side. I bit down hard on my mouth guard with each hit. Although I'd never been a fighter, I'd seen enough hockey fights on TV to know that the person on top would be the winner. As I arched my back and pushed down on him as hard as I could, I wondered how my mom was reacting from the stands. That's when I felt a hand on my back.

"Break it up, boys!" the ref ordered.

I felt him dig his hands between us and start to pry us apart. The ref pulled me to my knees, and I noticed that I'd knocked the helmet off the Spitfire player. He lashed out at me again and I swung right back.

"Separate!" the ref demanded.

I got to my skates, and the ref, holding the other player, pointed me toward the penalty box. Feeling a toxic rush of emotions and adrenalin, I glided with my head down toward the open door.

William skated by with one of my gloves and my stick. "Never seen you do anything like that before."

I nodded my head.

He left when the ref showed up. "I'm giving you a five-minute penalty. You're lucky it's not a suspension."

I flumped down in the penalty box, wondering why the ref didn't give me a league suspension. I had earned it.

15 TIME OUT

The game continued, and I glanced at the Spitfires player in the other penalty box. I felt bad that he'd had to receive the brunt of my frustration. I heard a tap on the glass and turned to see my mom, followed by my dad.

Her eyes bulged out of her head. "Tyler! What was that?"

She didn't have to speak loudly for me to hear her through the Plexiglas. I didn't have an answer she would've liked anyway. It was just a fight. A hockey brawl.

"That's the kind of stupid thing that'll ruin your hockey reputation! What coach is going to want to work with a kid like that?" she yelled.

"I wasn't suspended or anything." I did what I did, and I wanted to be left alone. The box was supposed to be a private place to sulk, but she wasn't done letting me have it.

"I sacrifice so much so you can play. All those early

mornings, hockey league committee board meetings, countless hours in cold arenas — all for you, and then you go and do something like this."

My dad interrupted. "I understand that you must be feeling very frustrated after hurting your knee."

His soft approach went down in flames, but I used it as a springboard. This was a now-or-never moment. I turned to face them directly. "I did it on purpose."

"What?" they yelled out in unison.

A few people in the stands who were trying to watch the game turned to give them a dirty look. Finally, after everything I'd tried, I had my mom's attention.

"I tried to hurt myself on purpose! That fight — same deal."

My dad needed confirmation. "Are you serious?"

"Yes!" I paused, collecting my words carefully. "I don't want to be the hockey player you want me to be. I want a life." They both stared at me. "I tried to hurt myself so I could get out of playing hockey."

"Excuse me?" my mom said, her hands digging into her sides.

My dad held out his hand. "Just let him speak."

"I'm tired of hockey. I don't want to play Double-A — I barely want to play Select right now. Hockey used to be fun, but not anymore. I just need a break."

My mom muttered, "We thought this was what you wanted."

My voice was empty of emotion. I was exhausted.

"I did. But not anymore."

"What *do* you want?" my dad asked.

"To not have to go to summer hockey camp. Maybe I can go to regular camp this year."

They were both silent. But I figured while we were on the topic, I would go for broke. "I want to hang out with friends, and I want to try other sports. And, it would also be nice to go to Canada's Wonderland a few times. We can pretty much walk there from our house."

My mom responded first. "So you're saying you're done with hockey. Finished. Just like that."

"No. I don't know. I love hockey. But giving something up because *I* want to is very different than giving something up because *you* want it. I was stupid to try to hurt myself instead of talking to you, but I knew you wouldn't get what I was trying to say."

She kept digging. "But I thought all this was what you wanted."

"I did, too, but things change. I guess I've changed. I want to be able to go to a movie and not worry about getting up early for practice. And I don't want to have to go to every single practice. There *are* players who miss some." I guess I had more demands than I thought. *Whatever happens,* I thought, *however they take this, I feel better.* Before my mom could lay down her verdict, I asked, "You were a gymnast. Didn't you ever feel what I'm going through?"

"That was a long time ago."

My dad nudged my mom. She took a deep breath. "My parents never supported my gymnastics. They both worked, and there was never time for it. I could —" She stopped.

"What, Mom?"

My dad reached out his hand and she took it. "I could have gone far. I could have done something with my —"

She stopped even though I knew what she was going to say next. "I didn't know."

She looked at me. "I don't think about it very often anymore."

Looking into my mom's eyes, I saw the same eyes I'd seen in that picture: a teenager holding her medal proudly.

"I want what you want," my mom said quietly. "Do you want to go to a movie?"

I didn't think she was trying be funny, but it came out that way. I laughed. "I'm kind of stuck in here. Besides, I don't think the ref would let me go yet. I think I need to finish my penalty."

"That guy made first contact," my dad pointed out.

I smiled, appreciating the support.

"Well, then you better get back to the game," my mom said, "if you want to."

They turned to leave and I stopped them. "Hey, guys, do you mind taking a picture of me in the box? I want to remember this moment."

They smiled, and my dad snapped a photo with his cell phone. A moment later, my penalty ended as the Spitfires iced the puck. I moved from the box to the bench to rejoin my line.

On the bench, Connor turned to me. "Your game better shape up. You wouldn't be the first to be booted off a Select team." He spat with perfect precision through the bars of his face mask, hitting the ice. "I'm watching you!"

"You decided to stay?"

I turned to Glenn's voice. He was standing next to Madison in the first row of the stands.

She added, "Is that a good thing or a bad thing?"

"Good," I said. "It went so much better than I expected."

Connor interrupted. "Hey, sis, why are you talking to this loser?"

She ignored him. "Wow, Tyler," Madison smiled. "You did the impossible. You broke through to your mom."

I checked the game, making sure my line wasn't up. "And I couldn't have done it without the both of you." I turned to Glenn and said, "Sorry if I've been a jerk lately."

"The important thing," Glenn said, "is that you can talk about it."

I laughed.

Madison said, "So tell me you threatened them with something juicy."

"Didn't have to. They agreed to back off on the hockey pressure, and now I'm free to hang out tonight after the game if you guys want to."

"Can't," Glenn said. "You've got Select practice in the morning."

I laughed at him knowing my schedule better than me. "Maybe I won't go."

"What?" Madison added. "*You*, miss a hockey practice?"

"Why not?" I grinned. "I don't want to miss out on the best years of my life!"

"Good to have you back," Glenn said.

"Good to be back."

"Hey, bozo," Connor said. "We're up."

I stood and Madison stopped me. She turned my shoulders to face her, leaned over, and gave me a big hug. I turned to see Connor staring at me in shock. I smiled at him and jumped the board, excited to get my skates back on the ice and just have fun.